My Little Pony

Around EQUESTRIA!

LITTLE, BROWN & COMPANY

LB kids

Little, Brown and Company

Hachette Book Group
1290 Avenue of the Americas, New York, NY 10104
Visit us at lb-kids.com

LB kids is an imprint of Little, Brown and Company
The LB kids name and logo are trademarks of Hachette Book Group, Inc.

The publisher is not responsible for websites (or their content) that are not owned by the publisher.

First Edition: September 2016

My Little Pony: Welcome to Equestria! originally published in April 2013 by Little, Brown and Company

My Little Pony: Welcome to the Crystal Empire! originally published in September 2013 by Little, Brown and Company

My Little Pony: Welcome to Rainbow Falls! originally published in April 2014 by Little, Brown and Company

My Little Pony: Welcome to the Everfree Forest! originally published in October 2014 by Little, Brown and Company

My Little Pony: Hooray for Spring! originally published in January 2015 by Little, Brown and Company

My Little Pony: School Spirit originally published in July 2015 by Little, Brown and Company

My Little Pony: Crusaders of the Lost Mark originally published in February 2016 by Little, Brown and Company

Library of Congress Control Number: 2016937668

ISBN 978-0-316-39529-8

10 9 8 7 6 5 4 3 2 1

WOR

Printed in the United States of America

Around EQUESTRiA!

FEATURING

My Little Pony

Welcome to Equestria!

By Olivia London

"Hey, Spike!" Twilight Sparkle calls out as her favorite baby dragon and number-one assistant runs into the library.

"Hey, Twilight," he replies. "You got a letter from Shining Armor and Princess Cadance!"

"Well, what does it say?" Twilight asks excitedly.

Dear Twilight Sparkle,

As the new rulers of the Crystal Empire, we have received many warm invitations to visit towns throughout Equestria, including Ponyville! We are delighted to come visit you and your friends, and we look forward to seeing your new home. Until then, we promise to send postcards from our journey. See you soon!

Love always,
Shining Armor
& Princess Cadance

"Did you hear that, Spike?" Twilight cries out. "My brother and Princess Cadance are coming! I can't wait to tell everypony!"

From a tall tower in the Crystal Castle, Shining Armor and Princess Cadance see clear across their glittering kingdom.

"I will miss our home while we are away," Princess Cadance says, "but I am excited for our trip!"

"Me, too," Shining Armor replies. "We'd better get going!"

"That's true. Oh, I don't want to forget this gift for Twilight!" the princess says, slipping a package into her satchel.

The couple spend the rest of the morning saying farewell to all the Crystal Ponies in their kingdom.

Finally, it is time for them to board their flying carriage and take off!

After a short while, the newlyweds arrive at their first destination: Canterlot! The majestic city where they grew up was also the setting for their beautiful wedding. They are delighted to visit Princess Celestia and Princess Luna at Canterlot Castle, and enjoy some time in the city together.

CANTERLOT

Dear Twilight,

 We arrived in Canterlot today after a lovely send-off in the Crystal Empire. It was wonderful to enjoy Canterlot knowing that it is now safe from that evil Queen Chrysalis! We went to the derby to watch the races, and we spent the night with Princess Luna. She took us to the observatory in your old library, where we watched her raise the moon. Then we went into town to see some shops. Cadance remembered how much your friend Rarity loves fashion, so she picked up a little something special for her. Our next stop is Cloudsdale! We'll write again soon.

 Much love,

 Shining Armor (& Princess Cadance)

7

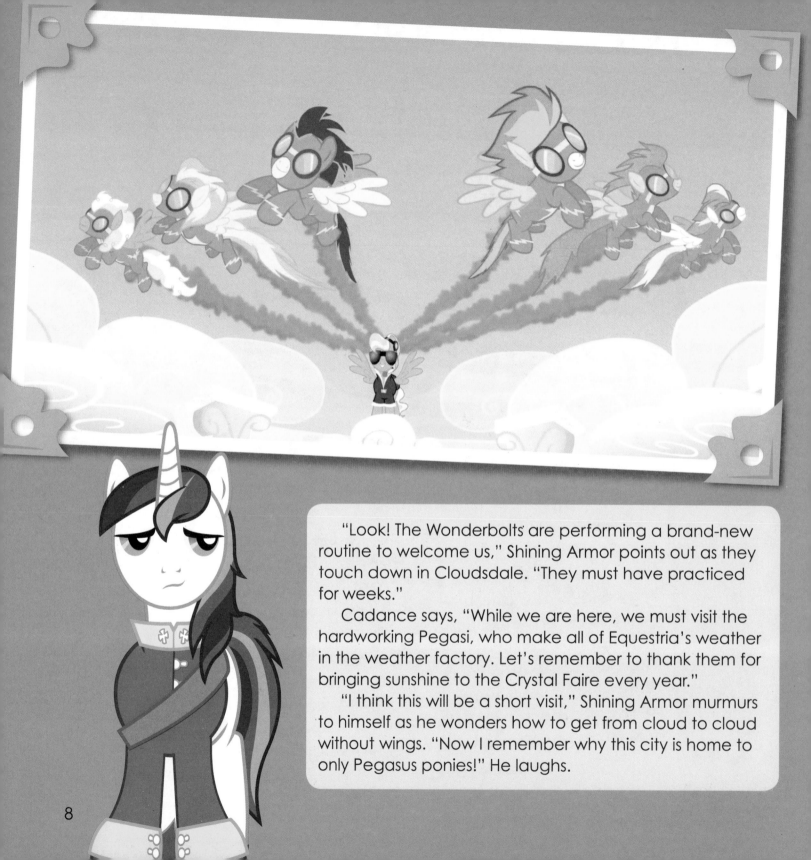

"Look! The Wonderbolts are performing a brand-new routine to welcome us," Shining Armor points out as they touch down in Cloudsdale. "They must have practiced for weeks."

Cadance says, "While we are here, we must visit the hardworking Pegasi, who make all of Equestria's weather in the weather factory. Let's remember to thank them for bringing sunshine to the Crystal Faire every year."

"I think this will be a short visit," Shining Armor murmurs to himself as he wonders how to get from cloud to cloud without wings. "Now I remember why this city is home to only Pegasus ponies!" He laughs.

CLOUDSDALE

Dear Twilight Sparkle,

    Today we arrived in Cloudsdale just in time to judge the Best Young Flyer competition. Being here reminds us of the time when your friend Rainbow Dash won the grand prize by performing a Sonic Rainboom. It must have been thrilling! I found something that made me think of her and will bring it with us to Ponyville. Looking forward to seeing you soon!

    Always,

    Princess Cadance (& your loving brother)

"Our next stop is Appleloosa," Shining Armor tells Cadance, looking down at the map.

"Yes, Applejack told me all about Appleloosa at our wedding," Cadance remembers. "It is a small town best known for its delicious apple orchards. And it took the ponies there only one year to build it!"

"That's impressive," says Shining Armor. "Doesn't Applejack's cousin Braeburn live here?" Cadance nods.

When the couple arrive, the town of Appleloosa is decorated in their honor, and Braeburn shows them around.

APPLELOOSA

Dearest Twilight,

   The orchards of Appleloosa are in full bloom, and Braeburn has been an incredibly gracious host. He says to tell you that the ponies and buffalo are still getting along well. We saw the tree that Applejack planted when you and your friends came to visit, and we are bringing her a little something special from one apple orchard to another! It's time for us to get going now. More later...

Your loving brother,
Shining Armor

"We have a very busy schedule in Manehattan," Princess Cadance tells her beloved as they fly over the city skyline toward their next stop. "We've been invited to a gala every night! This really is the most cosmopolitan city in all of Equestria. The *Manehattaner* will have reporters following us everywhere."

Shining Armor isn't as interested in the parties. "Let's ride the underground pony express train—it's called the Maneway," he says.

12

MANEHATTAN

Dear Twilight,

Manehattan is a very impressive city. The buildings are as tall as the sky, and the society is very sophisticated. But all the ponies here rush around like they're in a hurry! It's a bit fast-paced for us.

We tried some of the most delicious pastries we have ever tasted and knew at once that we must bring a treat for Pinkie Pie, who is so fond of sweets. We are now only a few short stops away from Ponyville!

Love,
Princess Cadance

The next few days are a whirlwind of adventure. They visit the town of Dodge Junction, the city of Fillydelphia, and Las Pegasus. In each town, the newlyweds and new leaders of the Crystal Empire are welcomed with open arms and a lovely party.

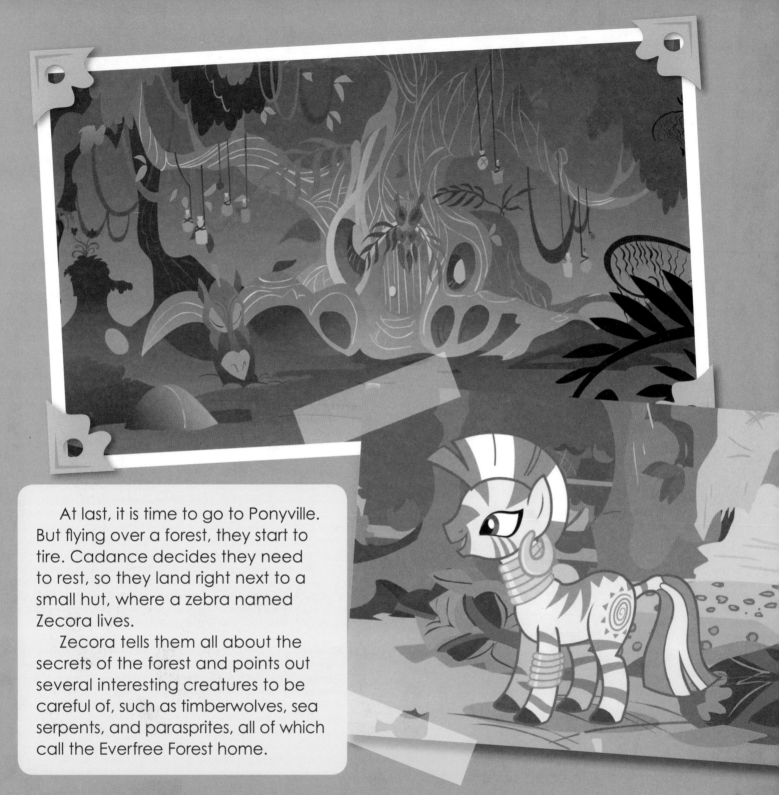

At last, it is time to go to Ponyville. But flying over a forest, they start to tire. Cadance decides they need to rest, so they land right next to a small hut, where a zebra named Zecora lives.

Zecora tells them all about the secrets of the forest and points out several interesting creatures to be careful of, such as timberwolves, sea serpents, and parasprites, all of which call the Everfree Forest home.

Dear Twilight,

Today we made a surprise stop in the Everfree Forest and had the most interesting day. Did you know that the forest doesn't work like the rest of the land? The plants and animals in the forest all fend for themselves. Clouds here can even move without the Pegasus ponies' help! We met someone who asked us to bring a special package to Fluttershy.

Anyway, we enjoyed our detour very much, but we will arrive in Ponyville tomorrow!

Love,
Shining Armor

The next day, Twilight and the mayor of Ponyville are already waiting for them in the town square.

"Welcome, Your Majesties," says the mayor.

"I'm so happy you're here!" Twilight cries out to them.

"Hi, Twilight," Shining Armor says, giving his little sister a hug.

"It's so good to see you," Cadance says with a swish of her tail.

"Are you ready to tour Ponyville?" Twilight asks, already leading the way. "This is the town square, and Ponyville Park, and the Day Spa. And there's the marketplace, where many ponies sell their goods. And this is Golden Oak Library— it's where Spike and I live. Come inside!"

"Would you like to see where all my friends live?" Twilight asks them.

"We would love to," Cadance replies, "and we can give them the gifts we picked up for them on our journey. But before we go, this is for you, Twilight. It's something from our home, so that you will always have a piece of us with you."

"Thank you!" Twilight shouts with glee. She unwraps a photograph of her brother and new sister-in-law in a hoofmade frame. "I love it!"

They set out to see the other ponies. "This is where Rainbow Dash lives. She controls our weather with the help of her fellow Pegasi," Twilight explains at the first house, which they have to get a lift to.

Shining Armor gives Rainbow Dash her gift: a pair of official Wonderbolts flying goggles.

"Thanks. This is awesome!" Rainbow Dash yells, putting on the goggles.

"This is SugarCube Corner, where Pinkie Pie lives. Downstairs is the bakery, where she works," Twilight says next.

"And this is the most decadent cupcake you'll ever taste," Princess Cadance says to Pinkie. "We had one in Manehattan and thought of you."

"Oh, thank you! I can't wait to eat it!" Pinkie Pie replies, jumping up and down. She sneaks a lick of the frosting. "Mmmmm!"

"This is Rarity's dress shop, the Carousel Boutique!" Twilight says, stopping in the store.

"Hello," Rarity greets them. "What an honor to have you in my shop."

"I thought you could make some use out of these fine new silks that just arrived at the fabric shop in Canterlot when we were there," the princess says, handing them to Rarity.

"Oh, thank you, Princess! I'm going to design some fabulous new couture with these!" Rarity coos. "Maybe you will wear one to a royal ball someday!"

"Here's Fluttershy's cottage," Twilight tells them.

"It's nice to see you again," Fluttershy greets them.

Shining Armor hands Fluttershy a small bottle. "On our journey, we visited the Everfree Forest and met your friend Zecora. She said this bottle of medicine would help your animals if they ever get sick."

"Oh, that's very kind of you," Fluttershy whispers.

"And this is Sweet Apple Acres. It's owned by Applejack and her family," Twilight says, leading Cadance and Shining Armor through the gate of a pretty farm.

"Welcome to Sweet Apple Acres!" Applejack calls out as she gallops up to them.

"Thank you," Shining Armor replies. "Your cousin was a wonderful tour guide in Appleloosa. We brought you a little something from an old friend: an apple from your tree, Bloomberg."

"Well, that's mighty nice of you both!" Applejack cheers.

"What a pretty town, Twilight," Cadance remarks. "No wonder you love it here."

"Ponyville is great," Twilight agrees. "But the reason I love it so much is because this is where I have so many friends. After all, isn't that what really makes a home?"

"You are much wiser than when you were a little foal," Cadance replies. "I am so proud of you." She gives Twilight a big hug.

Dearest Twilight,

We are finally home in the Crystal Empire, and while we are happy to be back, we miss traveling already! We had a wonderful time in Ponyville with you and your friends. Perhaps the next time we travel across Equestria, you could come with us. Until then, we look forward to having you and your friends as our guests here in the Crystal Empire, so please come visit us soon!

With love,
Princess Cadance & Shining Armor

Welcome TO THE CRYSTAL EMPiRE!

By Olivia London

"Hey, Spike," said Twilight Sparkle as she entered the library. "When did that scroll arrive?"

"Just a second ago," he answers, handing it to her.
"It's from Princess Cadance and Shining Armor!" Twilight cries in excitement.

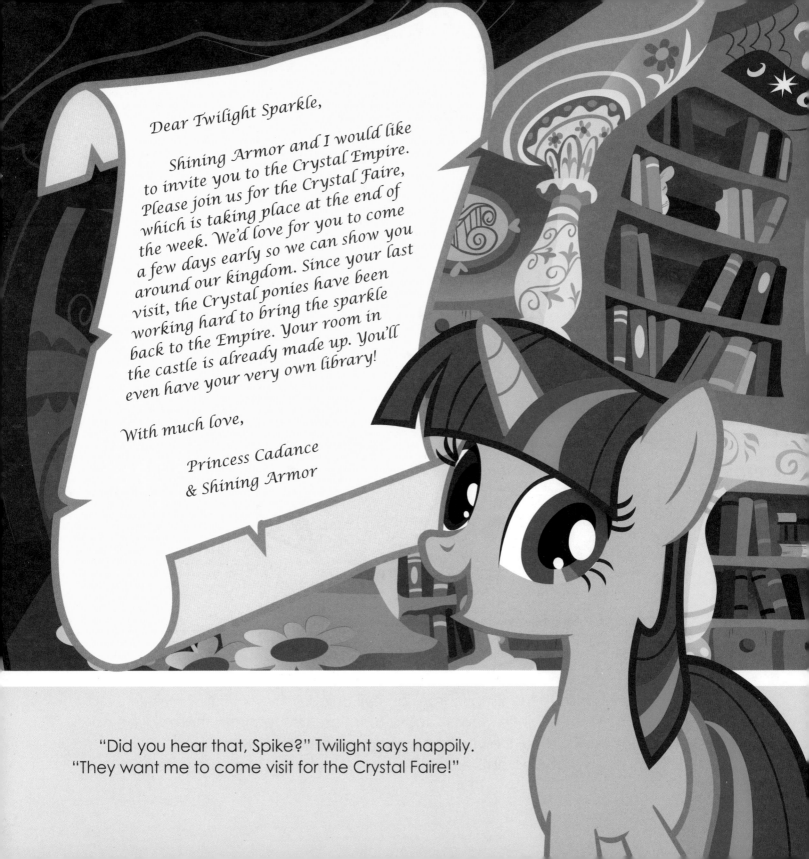

Dear Twilight Sparkle,

Shining Armor and I would like to invite you to the Crystal Empire. Please join us for the Crystal Faire, which is taking place at the end of the week. We'd love for you to come a few days early so we can show you around our kingdom. Since your last visit, the Crystal ponies have been working hard to bring the sparkle back to the Empire. Your room in the castle is already made up. You'll even have your very own library!

With much love,

Princess Cadance
& Shining Armor

"Did you hear that, Spike?" Twilight says happily. "They want me to come visit for the Crystal Faire!"

"It should be much more fun this time around," jokes Spike. "You know, now that you don't have to save the Empire from an evil Unicorn."

"That's for sure," Twilight agrees. "Not to mention that this time there will be no test from Princess Celestia. Do you remember how nervous I was?"

"Twilight, everypony remembers how nervous you were," Spike answers.

"Hmm, I guess I should start packing!" says Twilight. "Should I bring my books and my quills, just in case?"

"Promise you'll write to all of us about your trip?" Spike asks, jumping on top of Twilight's bag.

"I promise! Tomorrow, I'll say good-bye to all my friends, and then it's off to the Crystal Empire!"

27

The next morning, Twilight meets her friends in the town square to say good-bye.

"Ooh, I can't wait to hear all about the party!" Pinkie Pie exclaims, bouncing up and down.

"Well, it's not exactly a party—it's a Faire," Twilight corrects her.

"Y'all be careful now, ya hear?" Applejack says.

"Are you sure you don't need company?" Rarity asks. "The Crystal Empire is gorgeous—I'm just *dying* to see it again!"

"I'm sorry, Rarity, but they invited only me," Twilight replies. "It's the first time since the wedding that we'll be together as a family. You can come with me next time, okay? Oh, and Rarity, would you check in on Spike for me?"

"Of course," Rarity says.

"Have fun, Twilight!" Rainbow Dash calls out.

"Write to us!" Fluttershy offers.

"I will, I promise. See you soon, everypony!"

With that, Twilight Sparkle sets off on her journey to the Crystal Empire.

29

Twilight settles into her seat on the train and stares out the window, thinking about the last time she rode this same train. She was on her way to save the Crystal Empire from the evil Unicorn, King Sombra.

"Boy, a lot has changed since my last trip," Twilight remarks to herself, taking out her quill and a piece of parchment.

Dear Spike,

I know I just left Ponyville this morning, but I miss you already! Riding the train to the Crystal Empire is bringing back so many memories. It's hard to believe there was a time when we didn't know the Crystal Empire even existed. I'm still amazed that Princess Celestia trusted me to help protect it. Thank goodness I had you there with me. Otherwise, I never would have succeeded. I'm looking forward to seeing the Empire back in its prime—the way it used to be before it was overtaken. I can't wait to arrive and be able to tell you all about it. More later!

XOXO,
Twilight Sparkle

"Shining Armor!" Twilight cries out, seeing her brother waiting for her by the train station.

"Twily, it's so great to see you!" Shining Armor says, overjoyed. "Welcome back to the Crystal Empire. This time I promise we're actually going to have some fun."

When they arrive at the castle, Princess Cadance greets Twilight with a warm embrace.

"Sunshine, sunshine, ladybug's awake. Clap your hooves and do a little shake!" the ponies sing out in unison, clapping their hooves.

"It's wonderful to see you, Twilight," Princess Cadance says. "Thank you for coming to visit us. I'm looking forward to showing you around our Empire—now that everything is back to normal."

"It's so great to be here," Twilight replies. "I can't wait!"

Princess Cadance and Shining Armor show Twilight to her room so she can settle in.

"This room is huge!" Twilight exclaims.

"Our home is your home," Shining Armor replies. "Don't forget to check out the library. We'll be back in a little while to take you into town."

After spending some time reading up on the history of the Crystal Empire, Twilight decides to write another letter home.

Dear Applejack,

I'm in a room so big it could probably fit all of Sweet Apple Acres! Okay, well, maybe not quite that big....I've just been reading through some of the Crystal Empire's history. It still amazes me that one thousand years ago, King Sombra overtook the Empire. Thankfully, he was overthrown and banished, but before he left he cast a curse on the Empire, which caused it to disappear! That's why no one knew it existed!

Princess Celestia told me that if the Crystal Empire is filled with love and hope, those feelings are reflected across all of Equestria. But if hatred and fear take hold, they spread across Equestria, too. Pretty heavy, huh? I'll write more later, I promise! Say howdy to everypony for me!

Always,
Twilight

35

"We thought we'd just take a walk around the center of town first," Shining Armor says to his sister.

"Sounds great!" Twilight replies. "When is the Crystal Faire?"

"It's in two days," Princess Cadance says. "The Crystal ponies have been preparing for it all week long. It is the first real Crystal Faire since the Empire was reinstated, so it's a very special occasion."

"The Crystal ponies have a long and cultured history," Shining Armor adds. "A thousand years is a lot of time to make up for!"

Dear Fluttershy,

   The kingdom is so...so sparkly! All the Crystal ponies are really shiny now that they've got their Empire back. Did you know that when meeting with special guests, it's traditional for rulers of the Crystal Empire to weave crystals into their manes? It's called a special ceremonial headdress! Maybe we'll get to see Princess Cadance wear one sometime. Anyway, it was fun seeing the preparations for the Crystal Faire. It reminded me of when we were all here trying to put the Faire together when the Empire was in danger. I'm so lucky to have you ponies as my friends! Time to go to dinner now, more later.

                              Love,
                              Twilight Sparkle

"Rise and shine!" Shining Armor calls into Twilight's room the next morning. "I'm up, I'm up," she replies sleepily.

"Come on and get ready. We're going somewhere special this morning!" he announces.

"Hmm," Twilight says to herself. "I wonder where. . . ."

Dear Rainbow Dash,

Today was the best day ever! We went to a jousting match. It was so exciting—you would have loved it. The Crystal ponies have ancient, intricate sets of armor and an enormous stadium. It reminded me of when we were putting together the Crystal Faire. Next time, I promise you'll all come with me and we'll go to a match. I hope all is well in Ponyville! I'll write again soon.

Always,
Twilight Sparkle

It's the day of the Crystal Faire, and Twilight Sparkle is bursting with excitement!

"Twily, it's time!" Shining Armor calls to her.

When they reach the town square, the Faire is just beginning and the place is filling quickly with Crystal ponies from all over the Empire.

"You can really feel the love and light spreading," Twilight remarks.

"That is the purpose of the Faire," Princess Cadance offers in agreement.

"Yes, I remember!" Twilight replies. "The light and love of the ponies power the Crystal Heart, which protects the Empire from harm! This time I hope the real Crystal Heart is on display."

"Thanks to you and your friends, Twilight, the Crystal Heart is here to stay," Princess Cadance replies.

"Shall we go join in the activities?" Shining Armor says, heading for the Crystal berries booth.

Dear Pinkie Pie,

Today was the Crystal Faire! It was full of colorful tents and booths with games, fortune-telling, crafts, a petting zoo, and tons of food! They had every kind of pie imaginable! Crystal Empire Berry Pie, Crystal Apple Pie, Crystal Peach Pie, Crystal Chocolate Pie—you name it! And this time, the real Crystal Heart was there, and it was spectacular! All the love and happiness from the ponies lit it up, and it shot rainbow sparkles into the air! Next Faire, you're all coming with me. I can't wait to come home and tell you about it.

XOXO,
Twilight Sparkle

P.S. I tried to play the flügelhorn, but I think I still need some practice. . . . Next time, you'll have to show me how it's done!

41

Dear Rarity,

We went to the most luxurious spa this afternoon. You would have loved it! They have a special pool called the Crystal Mud Bath that relaxes your body and rejuvenates your coat. Speaking of sparkly coats, I also spent time talking to lots of Crystal ponies. They are all so much happier now that the Empire is safe. Do you remember when we were here last time? Their coats were so dull because King Sombra had erased their memories and stripped them of their love and light. Did you know it's that special magic that makes their coats sparkle so brightly? Next time we come here, I promise you'll have time to go into some of the fashion boutiques—I just know you could make something fabulous with their shiny crystal fabric. See you soon—I'll be home tomorrow!

Love always,
Twilight Sparkle

When morning comes, it's time for Twilight to say good-bye to Shining Armor and Princess Cadance.

"Thank you so much for having me," Twilight says, getting ready to board the train. "I had the most amazing visit!"

"It was our pleasure," Princess Cadance replies.

"Don't be a stranger, okay?" Shining Armor says, giving Twilight a hug.

Dear Princess Celestia,

My trip has made me think a lot about what happened when the Empire needed saving. I wanted to thank you for trusting me. I understand now more than ever how special the Crystal Empire is and how important it was to make sure that King Sombra did not overtake it again. It was a huge task, and I'm eternally grateful that you had faith in my ability to find the Crystal Heart and return it to the ponies of the Crystal Empire. And thank you for letting my friends come with me—sometimes we all need a little help, and I couldn't have saved the Crystal Empire without theirs. I'm so excited to go back with them soon!

          Your faithful student,
          Twilight Sparkle

"It's so great to be home!" Twilight Sparkle says, giving hugs to all her friends. "I had such a wonderful time, but I missed you ponies."

"We missed you, too, Twilight!" they all say happily.

Twilight looks around at everypony. "You really are my very best friends."

Welcome to Rainbow Falls!

Adapted by Olivia London

Based on the episode "Rainbow Falls" written by Corey Powell

45

"Twilight!" Spike calls, bursting through the front door of the
Golden Oak Library with a scroll tightly gripped in his claw.
"We got an official letter from the mayor of Ponyville!"

"Really?" Twilight Sparkle cries out, dropping the encyclopedia
she is reading and rushing to greet her best friend. "Well, open it
and see what it says!"

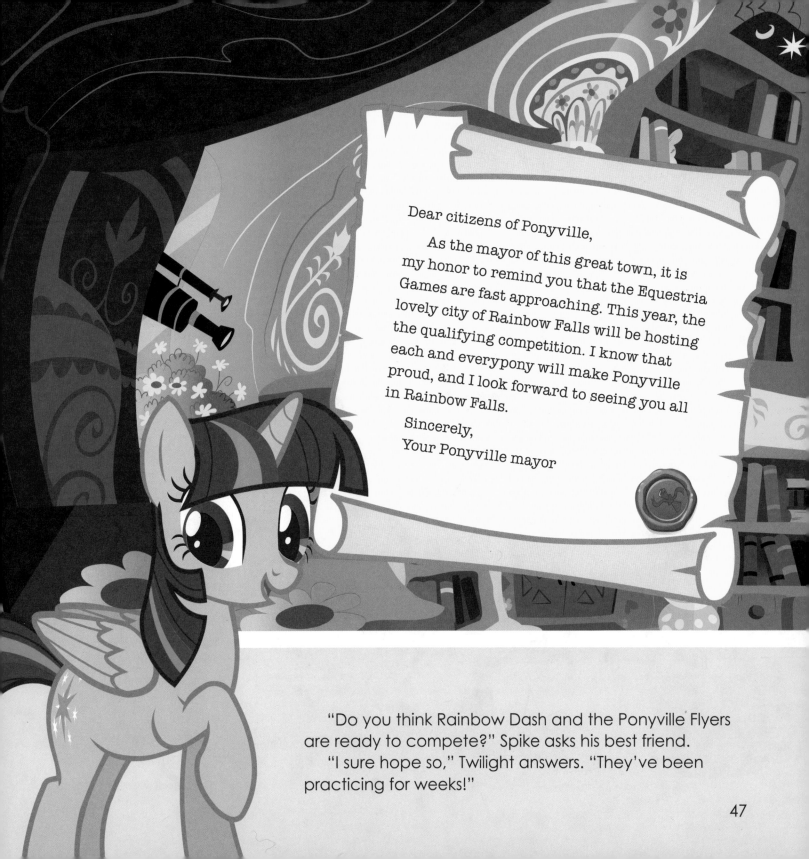

Dear citizens of Ponyville,

As the mayor of this great town, it is my honor to remind you that the Equestria Games are fast approaching. This year, the lovely city of Rainbow Falls will be hosting the qualifying competition. I know that each and everypony will make Ponyville proud, and I look forward to seeing you all in Rainbow Falls.

Sincerely,
Your Ponyville mayor

"Do you think Rainbow Dash and the Ponyville Flyers are ready to compete?" Spike asks his best friend.

"I sure hope so," Twilight answers. "They've been practicing for weeks!"

A few days later, it is time to leave for Rainbow Falls.

"Isn't this exciting, Spike?" Twilight remarks as she packs a few final things, including her travel guide. "I've never been to Rainbow Falls before! I can't wait to learn all about it."

"I wish I could come with you," Spike says longingly.

"I do, too," Twilight replies. "But Fluttershy is trusting you to watch over all her sick animal friends while we're gone, and that's a much more important responsibility."

"You're right!" Spike says. "I'm going to be the best critter-sitter ever!"

"That's the spirit!" Twilight agrees. "I promise I'll send you lots of postcards."

"Thanks, Twilight. I'll miss you!"

"Aww, I'll miss you, too, Spike!" she says, giving her friend one last hug before heading out the door. "See you in a few days!"

"All aboard the Friendship Express!" the conductor calls out over the loudspeaker. "All aboard!"

"I wonder what Rainbow Falls will be like," Fluttershy asks.

"I hear there are glorious, sparkling rainbows everywhere!" says Rarity.

"I hear the Rainbow Falls arena is enormous!" Rainbow Dash adds.

"Well, I hear they have a whole marketplace where ponies sell souvenirs and things for the games," Applejack begins. "I'm gonna set up my wagon there and sell my delicious apple brown Bettys to all the contestants."

Suddenly, everypony gasps and stares at Applejack.

"Don't worry, y'all!" she cries. "I'll make sure to save enough for you to load up on. I promise!"

The ponies let out a sigh of relief!

The friends are so busy talking that the hours fly by. Before they know it, the conductor makes an announcement.

"This station stop is Rainbow Falls! Watch your hooves while getting off the train! This stop: Rainbow Falls!"

"This is breathtaking!" Rarity remarks as she looks at hundreds of beams of light shooting down through the clouds, casting rainbows across the city.

The ponies leave the train station and head toward their hotel. On the way, they take in the beautiful rainbow scenery.

"It says here in my travel guide that Rainbow Falls was built on a cliff next to a waterfall," Twilight Sparkle tells her friends. "That's why there are always so many natural rainbows all over the town."

"Well, these Rainbow Falls ponies sure do make good use of them," Applejack says.

No more than a minute after dropping their bags in the room, Rainbow Dash announces, "Fluttershy and I are heading straight to the arena. We need to start practicing right away!"

Dear Spike,

Rainbow Falls is just as pretty as we all imagined! The ponies are so friendly, and they are very excited to be hosting the qualifying competition for the Equestria Games. Everypony left already to explore the city and start practicing for the races, but I stayed in the hotel to write to you, of course!

Our hotel is right in the center of the city. It's built into the side of a small waterfall, so the view from our room is really cool! Well, I'm off to go exploring now. I promise to write again soon!

XOXO,
Twilight Sparkle

Twilight Sparkle decides to explore the city of Rainbow Falls before joining the Ponyville Flyers in the Rainbow Falls arena, where they are practicing.

"'The Rainbow River, which runs all the way through Rainbow Falls,'" Twilight Sparkle reads aloud to herself, "'is one of the longest rivers in Equestria and—'"

Thump! With her head buried in the book, Twilight accidentally bumps into some ponies.

"Ouch!" comes a familiar squeak.

"Pinkie Pie? Rarity?" Twilight calls.

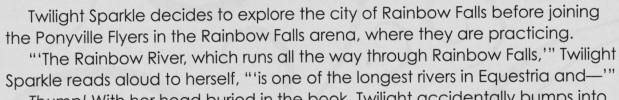

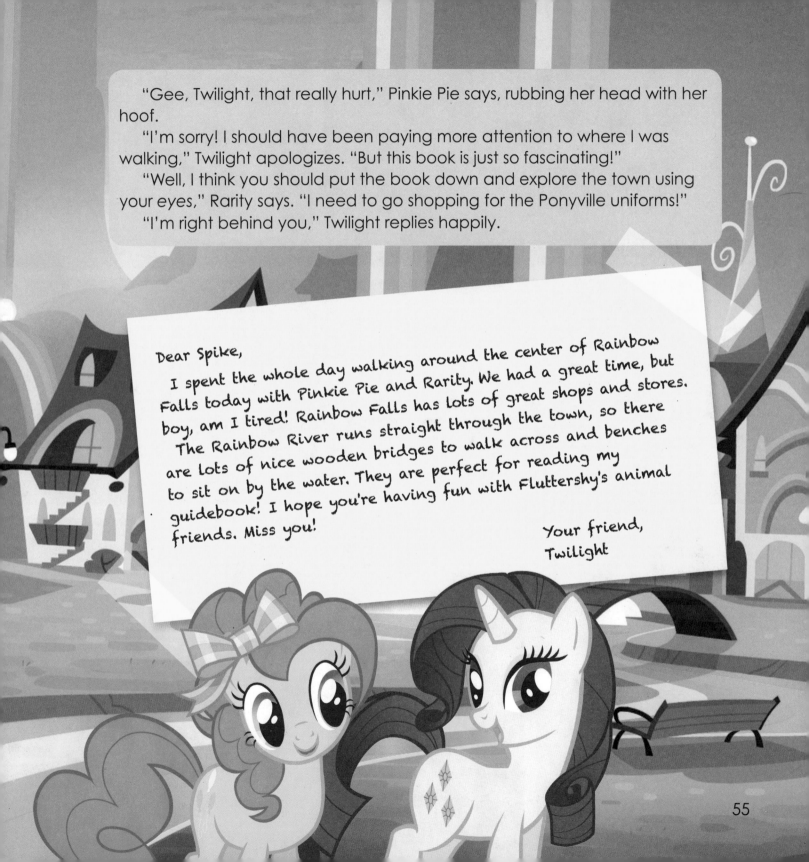

"Gee, Twilight, that really hurt," Pinkie Pie says, rubbing her head with her hoof.

"I'm sorry! I should have been paying more attention to where I was walking," Twilight apologizes. "But this book is just so fascinating!"

"Well, I think you should put the book down and explore the town using your eyes," Rarity says. "I need to go shopping for the Ponyville uniforms!"

"I'm right behind you," Twilight replies happily.

Dear Spike,

I spent the whole day walking around the center of Rainbow Falls today with Pinkie Pie and Rarity. We had a great time, but boy, am I tired! Rainbow Falls has lots of great shops and stores. The Rainbow River runs straight through the town, so there are lots of nice wooden bridges to walk across and benches to sit on by the water. They are perfect for reading my guidebook! I hope you're having fun with Fluttershy's animal friends. Miss you!

Your friend,
Twilight

The next day, Twilight Sparkle, Rarity, and Pinkie Pie get up early and head straight to the marketplace.

"Ooh, I can't wait to get some sweets," Pinkie Pie cries, jumping up and down.

"I hear they sell some marvelous beads and jewelry there, too," Rarity adds. "They will be the perfect finishing touches for my Ponyville uniforms."

"Did you know…" Twilight begins, her head stuck in her travel guide again. But Rarity and Pinkie Pie have already stopped listening.

"Get yer warm, delicious apple brown Bettys here! It's a Sweet Apple Acres family recipe!" Applejack yells as Rainbow Falls ponies gather around to try this delicacy they've never heard of before.

"But it's not rainbow-colored," one of the Rainbow ponies whispers to her friend, unsure whether to try it.

"It's like a rainbow in your mouth!" the other replies, taking a big bite. "You have to try it!"

Soon, there is a line of Rainbow Falls ponies a mile long, waiting to try Applejack's Bettys!

"I told y'all they'd be a hit here!" Applejack says.

"Shees ahhar dewishwush!" Pinkie Pie says, her mouth exploding with Bettys.

58

Dear Spike,

Today we spent the day in the Rainbow Falls marketplace. It's a lot like the marketplace in Ponyville, actually. This is where all the Rainbow Falls ponies come to set up their carts and wagons and sell their goods. Ponies were selling rainbow ribbons with medals on them, rainbow glasses, rainbow flags, rainbow horns and megaphones, rainbow foam hooves, rainbow pennants, and unicorn horns—all in honor of the Equestria Games qualifying competition. There were also lots of food carts, and Applejack set up her wagon and sold her apple brown Bettys—which were a huge hit! My first stop tomorrow is the Rainbow Falls arena to watch the Ponyville Flyers practice. Keep up the good work with the animals, and I'll write again soon.

Lots of love,
Twilight

"Okay, Flyers, let's try this one more time!" Rainbow Dash shouts at the top of her lungs.

"Wow, the Rainbow Falls arena is huge!" Twilight Sparkle comments, looking around.

"I know!" Rainbow Dash agrees. "It's the perfect place to practice—now, if Fluttershy and Bulk Biceps could just pass the horseshoe without dropping it, we'd be in business."

"It says in my travel guide that the Rainbow Falls arena was built by the same ponies who built the arena in the Canterlot Castle!" Twilight explains. "And, there are over twenty small tents set up along the sidelines so that each city has its own private area for contestants to wait their turn before competing."

"That's nice, Twilight," Rainbow Dash says, "but if you don't mind, we're trying to concentrate here. The race is only a day away."

"Oh, of course, don't mind me," Twilight replies, stepping away to write a postcard.

Dear Spike,

I spent the day in the Rainbow Falls arena watching everypony practice for the qualifying race. It was so exciting! The arena is enormous, and it's covered from one end to the other in shimmering grass that's the exact same length the whole way across! It says in my book that landscapers groom and measure the grass on the grounds twice a day to make sure it stays in perfect condition. There are all these giant reeds, hoops with horseshoes, arrows, and clouds with rainbows at the top set up all over the arena for the flying relay race. Rainbow Dash and Fluttershy have been practicing so much, I hope they make it! Well, I'm off to go watch them practice some more, but I'll write again to let you know how the qualifying match goes!

Your best friend,
Twilight

That afternoon, the ponies are still at the arena watching practice when one of the Wonderbolts hurts his wings.

"Oh no, it's Soarin!" the Cloudsdale ponies cry out. "Are you okay?"

"I'm hurt," he replies. "I think I need a medic."

"I don't mean to eavesdrop," Twilight cuts in, "but it says here in my travel guide that Rainbow Falls has one of the most advanced hospital facilities in all of Equestria. Maybe we should take him there?"

"That's a great idea!" Pinkie Pie chimes in. "We'll take him for you—we know you probably need to keep practicing."

"Thank you so much," the Cloudsdale ponies reply. "You Ponyville ponies are so friendly and helpful."

"I bet you didn't expect to explore the hospital on your tour of the city," Pinkie Pie says to Twilight as they wait for Soarin to get settled into a bed.

"I can't say that I did," Twilight replies. "But I'm glad we came. My guidebook says that Rainbow Falls Hospital was built with state-of-the-art machines and the latest technological equipment, so I'm sure Soarin is in the best hooves here."

Pinkie Pie and Twilight Sparkle stay until Soarin is all tucked in and feeling better. Then they head back to their hotel to get a good night's sleep. After all, the qualifying competition is tomorrow!

On the day of the competition, the Rainbow Falls arena is full of excitement. Tension is in the air as all the ponies gather on the grounds. The stands up above are full of ponies looking on and cheering for their teams, while the contestants are huddled in their cities' tents, getting ready to compete.

Finally, it's time for the Ponyville Flyers to compete in the relay race competition.

"I'm so nervous, I can hardly breathe," Rarity says to her friends from up in the stands.

"Go, Ponyville, go!" Pinkie Pie cheers, shaking her pom-poms.

"I hope Fluttershy and Bulk Biceps pass the horseshoe without dropping it this time..." Twilight says worriedly.

"So do we!" her friends agree.

Dear Spike,

Ponyville qualified! Fluttershy and Bulk Biceps were great and didn't drop the horseshoe once, and Rainbow Dash was amazing! The second she had that horseshoe in her mouth, she soared through the arena, cruised past the obstacles, and raced onto the winner's platform. I'm so proud of her!

It looks like our trip to Rainbow Falls was a hit. This is a truly great city, but we're all excited to come home! We leave tomorrow. I can't wait to see you and hear about your time with the animals. 'Til then, it's time to go celebrate with the team.

Hugs,
Twilight

"It's great to be home, Spike!" Twilight cries out, giving her number one assistant a hug.

"I sure missed you, Twilight," Spike says. "Thanks for all your postcards. I almost felt like I was there with you."

"Since you couldn't come to Rainbow Falls this time, I decided to bring a little Rainbow Falls to you."

"Thanks, Twilight! You're the best!"

Dear citizens of Ponyville,

As mayor of this great town, it is my honor and privilege to announce that the Ponyville Flyers have qualified to compete in the Equestria Games relay race competition. All the ponies in Ponyville are so very proud of our contestants, and we can't wait to see them shine in the upcoming games in the Crystal Empire. Please join us for a celebration in the town square tomorrow at four o'clock in the afternoon to congratulate our team!

With much pride,
Your Ponyville mayor

Welcome TO THE Everfree Forest!

By Olivia London

"Twilight! Oh, Twilight!" Spike calls, running into the library. "You've been in here for hours! Come outside and play...please?"

"I'm sorry, Spike, but I can't," Twilight Sparkle answers, her head burrowed between two books. "I'm in the middle of something very important."

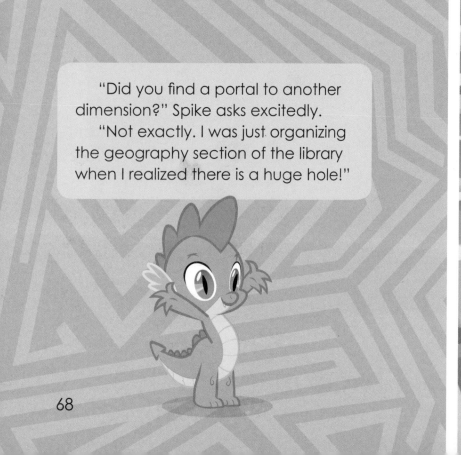

"Did you find a portal to another dimension?" Spike asks excitedly.

"Not exactly. I was just organizing the geography section of the library when I realized there is a huge hole!"

"Where? Let me see!" Spike cries out, jumping up. "Maybe it *is* a portal!"

"It's not that kind of hole, Spike," Twilight says.

"Oh. How many different kinds of holes are there?"

"I mean there's a gap in the *information*," Twilight explains. "I have absolutely nothing about the Everfree Forest in here."

"Good," Spike replies. "The Everfree Forest is spooky, and no one should ever go there."

"Without going into the Everfree Forest, I never would have found the Elements of Harmony and been able to save Equestria from Nightmare Moon," Twilight reminds him.

"I guess that's true," Spike agrees.

"I learned a lot about the Everfree Forest from that experience," she says. "In fact, we all did...."

"I know that look, Twilight," Spike says. "You've got an idea!"

"I sure do, Spike," Twilight replies. "Come on! Let's go!"

Twilight and Spike gather their friends together.

"What do you want to talk to us about, Twilight?" Applejack asks.

"I was organizing my library today and realized there's one subject missing from my Equestria section. I need your help to write a book about it."

"Oh my," says Rarity. "I've always wanted to write a book!"

"Is it about the history of the Wonderbolts?" shouts Rainbow Dash.

"Sorry, Rainbow Dash," Twilight says, shaking her head.

"So what *is* it about?" Pinkie Pie asks.

"The Everfree Forest."

There is a rush of murmurs and gasps.

"That Forest is just so dreadful!" Rarity cries.

"But we've all been inside it! We know it best. Sure, it's a little scary, but it should still be remembered as an important part of Equestria," Twilight explains.

"Come on, y'all," Applejack says. "Twilight needs our help!"

The ponies each write a section of the book.

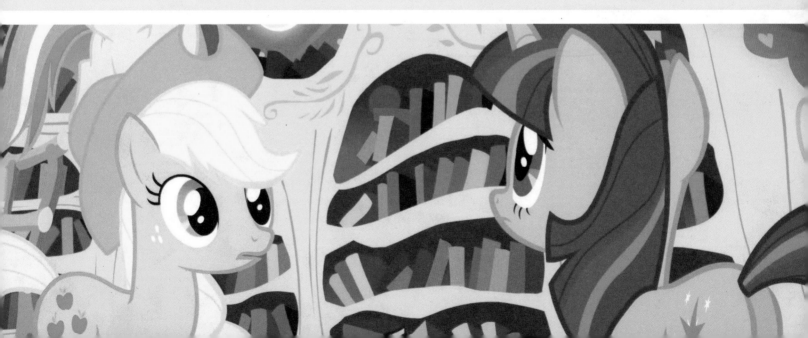

An Introduction to the Everfree Forest
By Twilight Sparkle

When I first moved to Ponyville, I came to oversee the Summer Sun Celebration. I had read about the prophecy of Nightmare Moon and how she would bring nighttime to all of Equestria—forever! The only thing that could save Equestria was reuniting what were known as the Elements of Harmony: Kindness, Laughter, Generosity, Honesty, Loyalty, and one mystery Element.

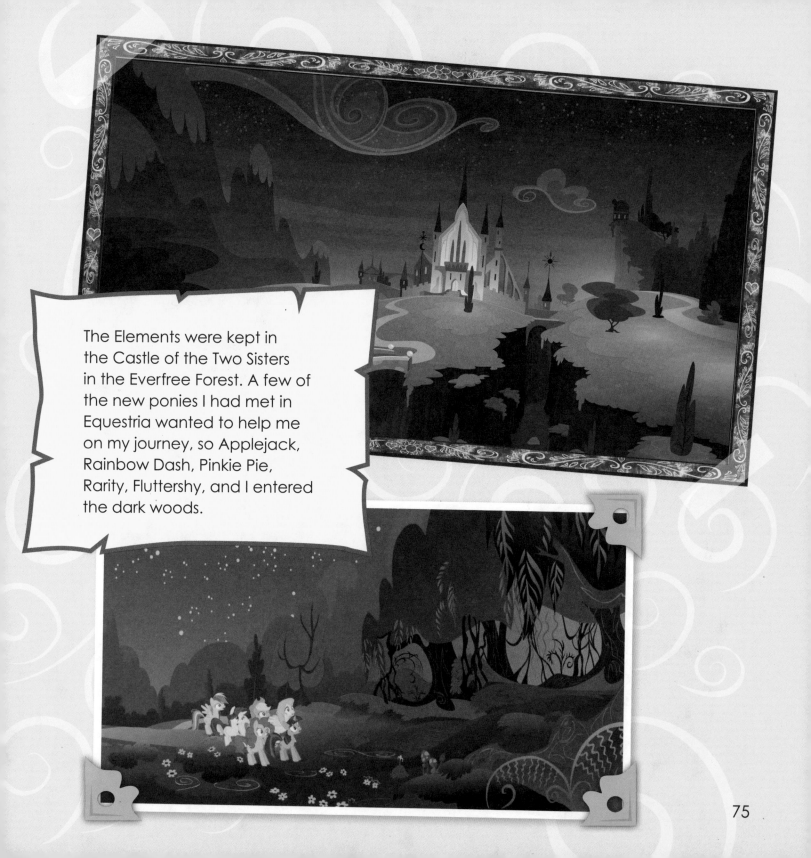

The Elements were kept in the Castle of the Two Sisters in the Everfree Forest. A few of the new ponies I had met in Equestria wanted to help me on my journey, so Applejack, Rainbow Dash, Pinkie Pie, Rarity, Fluttershy, and I entered the dark woods.

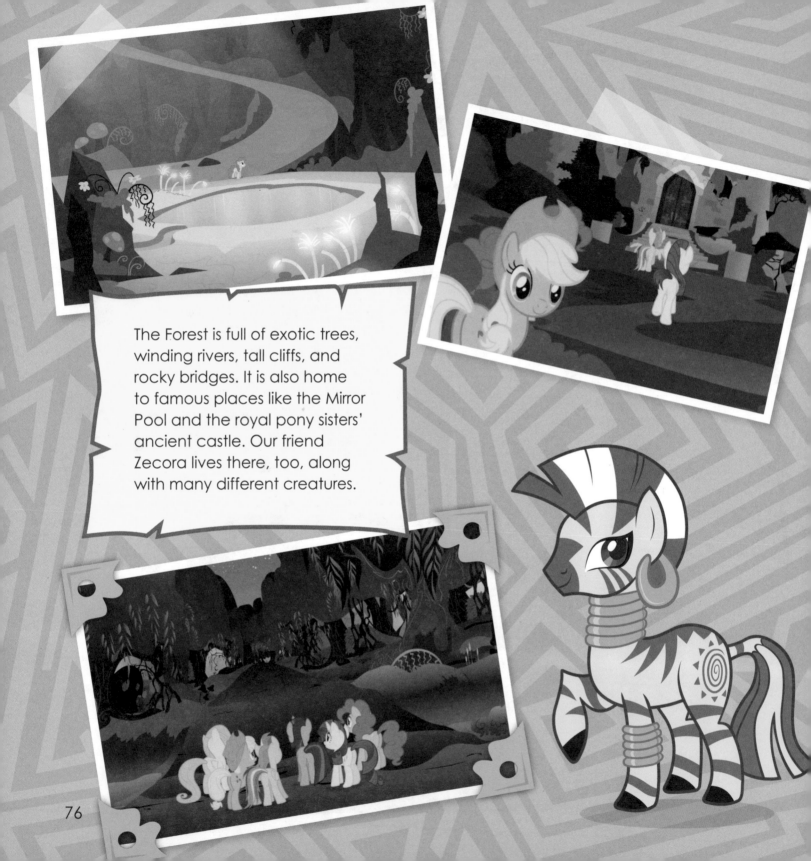

The Forest is full of exotic trees, winding rivers, tall cliffs, and rocky bridges. It is also home to famous places like the Mirror Pool and the royal pony sisters' ancient castle. Our friend Zecora lives there, too, along with many different creatures.

The Castle of the Two Sisters, now in ruins, was home to Princess Celestia and Princess Luna when they were young. The castle held the Elements of Harmony and helped us discover the sixth Element—Magic. My friends are the only reason I am able to put together this booklet containing all the known information about the Everfree Forest.

The Creatures of the Everfree Forest
By Fluttershy
The Everfree Forest is home to many different kinds of animals.

The Manticore

Manny Roar, a manticore, is a large creature with the body of a lion, the tail of a scorpion, and the wings of a dragon. He seemed awfully scary when we first met him, but he was just in pain! Poor thing had a splinter in his paw. After I removed it, he was the sweetest thing ever.

Parasprites

These tiny, adorable flying creatures look like bees but are much trickier to handle! They devour crops and multiply rapidly, just by coughing! They almost took over our town, until Pinkie Pie cleverly led them back into the Forest with music. Now we know never to take them out of their habitat—or feed them anything!

Ursas

These magical bears with fur that looks like the night sky live deep in the Forest. Ursa Major is the mother; Ursa Minor is the baby. It appears that when they are left alone, they keep to themselves.

Timberwolves

These are by far the scariest animals in the Forest. They look like wolves, only they are bigger and more terrifying, with bright green eyes and an unstoppable hunger. They have been known to chase ponies when they are looking for their next meal! They have very foul breath, and if they break apart, they seem to come back even larger. Definitely beware of timberwolves!

The Cockatrice

This is a curious creature with the head of a chicken and the body of a snake. It has the mysterious ability to turn ponies and animals to stone. I can reverse its stoning effect with "the stare," my gift, but I can't always control it.

ZECORA AND THE SECRET PLANTS AND MEDICINES OF THE EVERFREE FOREST

BY APPLEJACK

A LONG TIME AGO, EVERYPONY WAS AFRAID OF ZECORA, THE ZEBRA WHO LIVES IN THE FOREST. WELL, EVERYPONY EXCEPT MY LITTLE SISTER, APPLE BLOOM. ONE TIME, APPLE BLOOM WENT TO TALK TO ZECORA AND PROVE EVERYPONY WRONG. WE FOUND HER AT THE EDGE OF THE FOREST NEAR A BLUE PLANT. ZECORA TRIED TO WARN US THAT THE PLANT WASN'T SAFE, BUT WE THOUGHT SHE WAS CURSING US! WE ALL TOUCHED IT AND CAME DOWN WITH MYSTERIOUSLY FUNNY SYMPTOMS. THE BLUE PLANT IS CALLED POISON JOKE, AND WHEN WE FOUND OUT IT WAS THE CAUSE OF OUR SICKNESS, BOY, DID WE FEEL SILLY! THAT'S WHEN WE LEARNED YOU SHOULD NEVER JUDGE A BOOK—OR A ZEBRA—BY ITS COVER.

POISON JOKE: THIS BLUE PLANT HAS A BULB IN THE CENTER AND LARGE BLUE PETALS. IT LOOKS LIKE A FLOWER AND LIKES TO PLAY PRACTICAL JOKES ON EVERYPONY WHO TOUCHES IT. WATCH OUT!

SEEDS OF TRUTH: THE FLOWER FROM THESE SEEDS IS THE ONLY KNOWN CURE FOR CUTIE POX, BUT IT WILL ONLY SPROUT FROM HEARING THE TRUTH. THEN, THE PETALS CAN BE EATEN.

The Dark That Lurks Inside the Everfree Forest
By Rarity

We're supposed to be finding nice things to say about the Everfree Forest, but I've found the place to be nothing but dreadful. It's dark and murky, and they say that everything in the Forest works on its own—without any help or forces from inside Equestria. Can you imagine!? The plants grow on their own, the animals take care of themselves, and even the weather changes without help from the ponies. It's just terrifying. I do my best to avoid it whenever possible—and you should, too!

I did meet that lovely sea serpent, Steven Magnet, in the Forest. He was swimming in the river, howling about his mustache. Someone had rudely cut half of it off, poor thing! Still, the Everfree Forest gives me the chills, and that's all I have to say. Now I have a very important dress to design. Ta-ta!

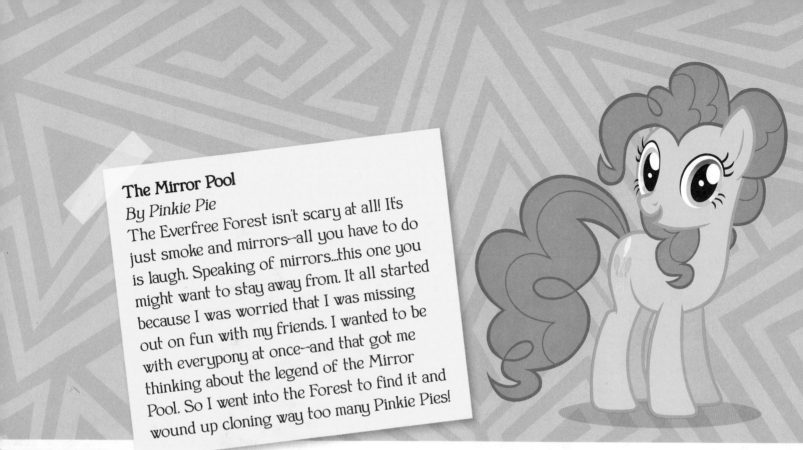

The Mirror Pool
By Pinkie Pie

The Everfree Forest isn't scary at all! It's just smoke and mirrors—all you have to do is laugh. Speaking of mirrors...this one you might want to stay away from. It all started because I was worried that I was missing out on fun with my friends. I wanted to be with everypony at once—and that got me thinking about the legend of the Mirror Pool. So I went into the Forest to find it and wound up cloning way too many Pinkie Pies!

Deep inside the Forest is a pool of magical water. When you recite a specific rhyme, a hole in the ground opens up and you fall through it. When you recite another rhyme, it activates the pool, which turns your reflection into a clone! It can be very dangerous, though, so we closed up the entrance to the pool for good. Still, the Everfree Forest is full of all kinds of cool things like the Mirror Pool. You should totally go inside and explore it!

Go On an Adventure!

By Rainbow Dash

This concludes our book on the Everfree Forest. You know everything that we know. You want a little danger in your life? You want to get the adrenaline pumping? Be brave. Take a walk through the Forest!

My Little Pony: Hooray for Spring!

Based on the episode by **Cindy Morrow**
Adapted by **Louise Alexander**

Twilight Sparkle leaped out of bed. "Hooray for spring!"

After months of cold temperatures and snow, it was finally time for Ponyville's Winter Wrap-Up!

Spike rolled over groggily. "Nooooo, let me keep hibernating," he said, pulling the covers over his head.

"Come on, Spike! Winter Wrap-Up is an annual tradition! I'm so excited to prepare Ponyville for sunshine and rainbows and flowers and animals!" Twilight gleefully checked off the items she needed for a hard day of work.

scarf

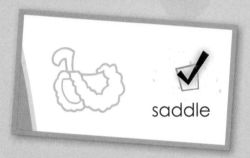

saddle

boots

Spike

Twilight finally roused Spike from his sleep, and they arrived at Town Hall just as the mayor of Ponyville called everypony to join Winter Wrap-Up.

"I need you to share your talents! We have a lot of work to do by the end of the day! You've each been assigned a team," said the mayor. "Weather team, your leader is Rainbow Dash!"

"Flight crew, let's clear out these clouds and bring sunshine back to Ponyville!" called out Rainbow Dash. "I'm also gonna need a group to guide birds back from the south."

A team of Pegasi gathered, eager to take off into the skies. Twilight looked at them with envy, wishing she was a natural flyer. Alas, she had no wings!

"Pinkie Pie needs help on the ground…er, ice," the mayor went on.

"Wheeeeeeeeeeeeeeeee!" Pinkie Pie slid by on a pair of ice skates.

"Ice crew, you slice the ice so when the sun comes out, it breaks up nice and neat," said the mayor.

Twilight looked nervously at the frozen lake. She had never been on ice skates before and didn't see a good reason to start a new sport *now*!

"Plant team, report to Applejack!" called the mayor.

"Okay, y'all," Applejack said. "We've got a lot of hard work ahead. I need the strongest ponies to pull plows and clear snow out of the fields!"

Big McIntosh and his friends stepped forward. "Eeyup."

"Great, Big Mac! Y'all will need a posse to plant seeds once the snow's gone. There are a lot of crops to grow!"

Twilight sighed. No way was she strong enough to drive a plow.

She didn't know what she'd be able to do without her magic, which wasn't allowed.

"Last but not least, the animal team follows Fluttershy," the mayor finished.

Fluttershy stepped up to the microphone bashfully. "Wake up our cute little friends from their long winter sleep, but be kind and gentle as we visit their homes."

Fluttershy continued. "Some of you will build nests with Rarity to welcome our feathered friends from the south."

Rarity held up a perfectly rounded bowl made of sticks and hay woven together with bright, shiny ribbons.

Spike whistled. "That's some fancy real estate for an egg!"

The mayor blew a whistle. "All right, ponies! Go awaken spring!"

As everypony followed their leaders, Twilight sighed.

"C'mon, Spike, we'll just have to see who needs us the most."

Fluttershy's team had the kindest and craftiest ponies. While Fluttershy gently called into every den to wake up sleeping critters, Rarity lovingly constructed elaborate nests.

Twilight noted they seemed to be moving a little too slow. There were still hundreds of nests to build and dozens more critters to awaken!

There was no doubt Rainbow Dash's team had the fastest flyers. But Twilight noticed there were still an awful lot of clouds in the sky. Without more sun, it would take forever to clear the snow.

Sure enough, even though Applejack's team had the strongest ponies, mounds of snow still covered the fields.

Twilight felt sad that she hadn't helped her friends. Plus, it seemed impossible that the ponies would be finished readying Ponyville to welcome spring before sunset.

As she stood thinking of the best way to help, the team leaders started arguing.

"Weather team, move those clouds faster," yelled Applejack. "I need more sun to melt that darn snow!"

"Simmer down, AJ," snapped Rainbow. "I can't work my team any faster. They're exhausted!"

"If anything, we should move *slower*," Fluttershy warned. "If we startle the animals, we'll scare them back into hibernation."

Twilight suddenly had a great idea. She whispered for Spike to fetch her clipboard.

"What is this fighting about?" the mayor demanded.

Applejack, Rainbow, and Fluttershy looked down, embarrassed.

"No problem here!" Twilight interrupted. "We were just reviewing the final checklists. AHEM, RIGHT, ponies?"

Twilight's friends nodded and turned to her for instructions.

"Ponies, it's time to do what I do best: Get organized!"

The ponies groaned.

"I know it might not sound fun to you, but making to-do lists and checking things off is *my* special talent. If we work together, I just know we can finish Winter Wrap-Up on time!"

For the next few hours, the ponies raced to finish their tasks. They formed an assembly line to build nests, skated in precise lines to cut the ice into a neat grid, and strung bells across the animal dens to wake them all up with a gentle alarm.

Just before sundown, the mayor called Twilight onstage.

"Before I pronounce the official arrival of spring, I want to thank Twilight Sparkle for helping everyone work together. From now on, she will be Winter Wrap-Up's All-Team Organizer!" Twilight put on a special vest.

Twilight blushed. "I couldn't have done it without my friends. Everypony worked so hard today!"

Suddenly, thousands of colorful birds filled the sky, trees blossomed with fragrant pink flowers, and bright rays of sunlight sparkled off the surface of the lake.

"Hooray for spring!" Twilight whooped.

"Hooray!" the ponies cheered. Twilight and her friends could not remember Ponyville ever looking so pretty.

Just when Twilight didn't think the day could be more beautiful, Rainbow Dash launched upward and produced a beautiful rainbow. Everypony looked in awe as it stretched across the sky.

"What a magical way to start spring." Twilight smiled.

Spike nodded in agreement. Then he curled up for a nap in a perfect puddle of sunshine.

School Spirit!

Adapted by **Louise Alexander**
Based on the episode "Ponyville Confidential" by **M. A. Larson**

The first day of school is over, and Sweetie Belle and Scootaloo are sad.
"I can't believe Featherweight got his cutie mark over summer vacation," Scootaloo says.

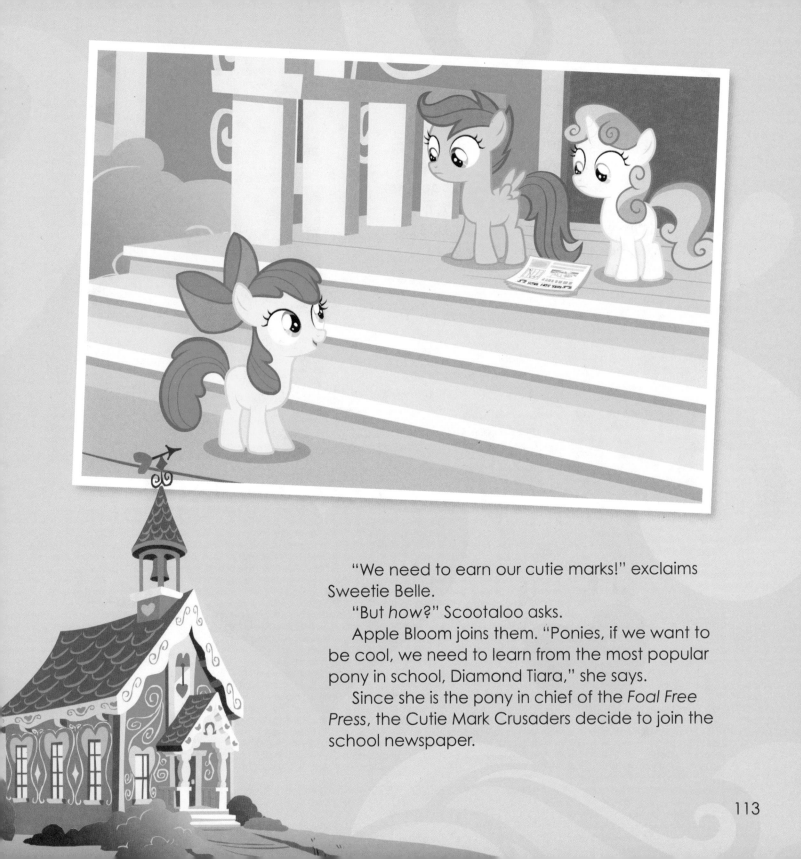

"We need to earn our cutie marks!" exclaims Sweetie Belle.

"But *how*?" Scootaloo asks.

Apple Bloom joins them. "Ponies, if we want to be cool, we need to learn from the most popular pony in school, Diamond Tiara," she says.

Since she is the pony in chief of the *Foal Free Press*, the Cutie Mark Crusaders decide to join the school newspaper.

At their first meeting, Sweetie Belle, Scootaloo, and Apple Bloom nervously listen as Diamond Tiara talks about her goals for the newspaper this year.

"I am going to deliver this paper to newfound glory! I want juicy stories—the juicier the better!"

Sweetie Belle, Scootaloo, and Apple Bloom spend the rest of the week writing their very first articles.

Apple Bloom loves history, so she talks to Granny Smith about the early years of Ponyville.

Scootaloo loves nature, so she writes a story about newborn animals.

Sweetie Belle loves fashion, so she interviews Rarity about her newest hat design.

The Cutie Mark Crusaders hand in their stories to Diamond Tiara, but the pony in chief throws the papers back in their faces.

"You call this news?!" she screeches. "Get something else on my desk by the end of the day! And it better be juicy!"

"How are we ever going to find other stories to write by the end of the day?" Scootaloo asks.

Suddenly, Sweetie Belle notices something funny and grabs Featherweight to take pictures.

They catch Snips and Snails sticking to a giant blob of bubble gum! Sweetie Belle knows the photo will make the whole school laugh— and she's right.

The lead story in the next *Foal Free Press* reads:

SNIPS AND SNAILS AND BUBBLEGUM TAILS

The story is by Gabby Gums, the name the Cutie Mark Crusaders use.

The next day, everypony in school is talking about the article! Snips and Snails pretend to be okay, but they are embarrassed.

Diamond Tiara, on the other hand, is thrilled! She congratulates the Crusaders.

"I want more! You are my new top gossip columnists!"

"We really have a gift for gossip, ponies!"
Scootaloo cheers as she high-hooves Sweetie Belle
and Apple Bloom.

Sweetie Belle replies, "If we write a few more
Gabby Gums articles, I know we'll earn our cutie
marks for sure!"

The trio sneaks around Ponyville, looking for more gossip.
Other articles appear in the *Foal Free Press* with crazy headlines:

TROUBLE IN PARADISE? LOUD CRYING HEARD COMING FROM HOME OF POUND AND PUMPKIN CAKE...

TRICKS UP HER SLEEVE! WE REVEAL THE GREAT AND POWERFUL SECRETS OF TRIXIE!

Soon, Gabby Gums isn't just the talk of Ponyville School, she's a hit all over Ponyville!

Piles of the *Foal Free Press* disappear as ponies line up to get the latest Gabby Gums gossip!

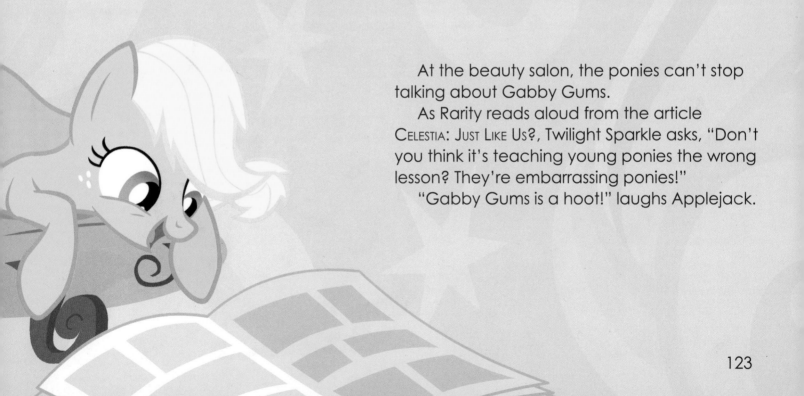

At the beauty salon, the ponies can't stop talking about Gabby Gums.

As Rarity reads aloud from the article CELESTIA: JUST LIKE US?, Twilight Sparkle asks, "Don't you think it's teaching young ponies the wrong lesson? They're embarrassing ponies!"

"Gabby Gums is a hoot!" laughs Applejack.

"I just think Gabby Gums should have more respect for other ponies' privacy! It's not nice to share embarrassing moments or secrets with the entire town!"

The other ponies roll their eyes at Twilight Sparkle.

At the same time, the Cutie Mark Crusaders are starting to feel bad about hurting ponies' feelings. They want to write about their interests again.

But Diamond Tiara will not let them. "We're even bigger than the *Ponyville Express* now!" she exclaims. "Gabby Gums needs to keep delivering the hottest stories in town!"

"Well," sighs Sweetie Belle, "if we want to earn our cutie marks, I guess we have to give the ponies what they want."

Later that week, ponies around town eagerly open the latest issue of the *Foal Free Press*. But their excitement turns to anger as they read the headlines:

PINKIE PIE IS AN OUT-OF-CONTROL PARTY ANIMAL!

APPLEJACK: ASLEEP ON THE JOB!

FLUTTERSHY HAS TAIL EXTENSIONS!

TWILIGHT SPARKLE: I WAS A CANTERLOT SNOB!

"This gossip has become just plain hurtful," says Twilight Sparkle.

Even Rarity has to agree with Twilight when she reads the next headline:

DRAMA QUEEN DIARIES: RARITY'S SECRETS REVEALED!

Suddenly, Rarity realizes that Sweetie Belle is Gabby Gums! Her sister has stolen her diary and published her secrets!

"Sweetie Belle, how could you do this to me?!" Rarity storms into her sister's room. "You're hurting people and invading their privacy! Gabby Gums's nasty news is making ponies feel horrible!"

Indeed, all over town, ponies start to ignore Sweetie Belle, Apple Bloom, and Scootaloo as word gets out that they are behind the Gabby Gums gossip column.

Sweetie Belle, Apple Bloom, and Scootaloo realize if being mean is what it takes to be popular, or to earn a cutie mark, it isn't worth it.

They want to apologize and get their friends back...and Sweetie Belle has a great idea how to do it.

The Cutie Mark Crusaders decide to tell the truth. Gabby Gums publishes her last column:

To the Citizens of Ponyville:

I want to apologize for the embarrassment I've caused. My column was actually written by Sweetie Belle, Apple Bloom, and Scootaloo. We got so swept up in earning our cutie marks that we forgot to be nice. But, ponies, we're changing our tune—we promise from now on to respect the privacy of others and not engage in harmful gossip. We hope you'll forgive us, Ponyville.

Signing off for the last time,

Gabby Gums

Sweetie Belle, Apple Bloom, and Scootaloo hand-deliver a copy of the paper with their letter to all the ponies they hurt. It feels good to get hugs from friends and family who accept their apologies.

School has just started for the year, but these ponies have already learned a lot!

CRUSADERS OF THE LOST MARK

Based on the episode "Crusaders of the Lost Mark"
by **Amy Keating Rogers**
Adapted by **Magnolia Belle**

Apple Bloom, Scootaloo, and Sweetie Belle are in their clubhouse reviewing what they've done to find their cutie marks.

"We've tried to do most everything, but if we keep tryin', we'll find our marks, Cutie Mark Crusaders!" Apple Bloom reassures them.

Pipsqueak runs into the clubhouse and shouts, "Cutie Mark Crusaders! I need your help! I'm running for student pony president against Diamond Tiara! Would you be my campaign managers?"

"We never tried getting our cutie marks in campaign managin' before. Let's do it, Crusaders!" Apple Bloom announces.

Soon after, students are gathered in the school yard listening to Pipsqueak speak.

"If I'm elected student pony president, I'll go to the school board and get our playground equipment all fixed up!"

"Oh yeah? Well, if Diamond Tiara is voted in, we will put a statue of her in the center of the school yard!" Silver Spoon says, scoffing at the other ponies.

Diamond Tiara pulls Silver Spoon aside and scolds her. "Silver Spoon! That was my big announcement for when I won!"

"Gosh, I'm sorry. I was only trying to help," Silver Spoon says sheepishly.

Diamond Tiara is annoyed. "Well, I don't need that kind of help!"

"Do we really want a big statue of Diamond Tiara, or would we rather have new playground equipment?" Scootaloo asks the other students.

Sweetie Belle rallies the ponies. "A vote for Pip is a vote for the playground!"

Since Diamond Tiara knows that the Cutie Mark Crusaders are swaying the voters, she tries to intimidate her fellow students.

"Vote for me," she cries, "unless you want all your secrets revealed!"

Silver Spoon tries to help Diamond Tiara again. "You can win the whole election if you just show the students that you really care...."

"I don't recall asking you to speak!" Diamond Tiara snaps at Silver Spoon, then storms away to vote.

The Cutie Mark Crusaders see that Silver Spoon's feelings are hurt. "When you're votin'," Apple Bloom says to her, "please consider voting for kindness and a pony who will listen."

Miss Cheerilee comes out of the schoolhouse. "The votes have been counted, and the results are in! The new student pony president is"—she pauses for suspense—"Pipsqueak!"

The students all cheer. "Hip, hip, hooray for President Pip!"

The Cutie Mark Crusaders look at their flanks, but they're still blank. They're disappointed they didn't get campaign manager cutie marks.

Diamond Tiara can't believe she lost the election. She asks Miss Cheerilee for a revote, since it's obvious to her the results are wrong.

The teacher feels bad for her student but tells her that Pipsqueak won fair and square.

Scootaloo is concerned about Diamond Tiara. "We should make sure she's okay."

"Yeah, just 'cause she's never cared about anypony else's feelings doesn't mean we shouldn't care about hers," Apple Bloom adds.

Diamond Tiara's mother, Spoiled Rich, is very upset about her daughter's defeat. "You mean I bought all these party supplies just to celebrate nothing?!"

Diamond Tiara sighs. "Sorry, Mother."

As she reflects on her actions, Diamond Tiara realizes her treatment of others impacted the vote. "I've made mistakes. I feel like a flawed diamond, but I just want to shine," she says.

"Poor thing. She wants to be better, but she doesn't know how," Apple Bloom laments over Diamond Tiara.

Sweetie Belle adds, "It seems like she could use a friend or two."

"Sounds like a job for the Cutie Mark Crusaders!" Scootaloo howls as all three raise their hooves.

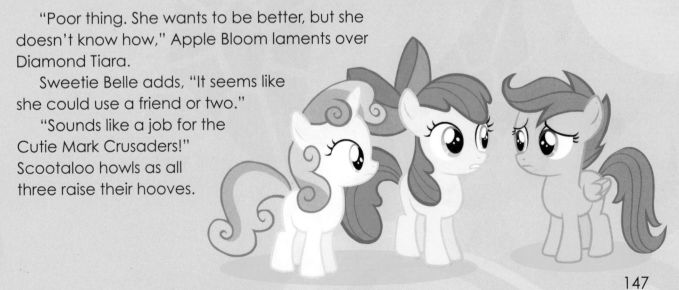

Diamond Tiara accepts an invitation to the Cutie Mark Crusaders clubhouse. She is astonished as she looks at their cutie mark charts.

"You three are...really lucky," Diamond Tiara tells them.

The Cutie Mark Crusaders are surprised to hear this. "We are?" they ask in unison.

"Well, yeah, you get to learn who you really are before you're stuck with a cutie mark you don't understand." Diamond Tiara seems sad.

"Aw, Diamond, you just need to be true to your cutie mark. You have such strong powers of persuasion. You can do great things!" Apple Bloom says.

From outside the clubhouse, Pipsqueak shrieks, "Cutie Mark Crusaders! There's no money in the school budget for new playground equipment! What do I do?"

"Don't worry, Pip! It'll be okay," Sweetie Belle reassures him. "We'll meet you back at school and help you find a solution!"

A grin flashes across Diamond Tiara's face. She bursts out of the clubhouse toward the school. The Cutie Mark Crusaders chase after her and remind her to be true to her cutie mark.

Diamond Tiara says, "You're working harder than anypony to get your cutie marks! I'm going to use my talent for persuasion to ask my father to donate money for the new playground!"

The Cutie Mark Crusaders watch proudly as brand-new playground equipment is delivered a few days later.

Apple Bloom wonders, "Maybe we should take some time off from worryin' about our cutie marks and help other ponies discover their true talents instead."

"Yeah, that's lots more fun and important than worrying about our own cutie marks!" Sweetie Belle exclaims.

Suddenly, a magic wind sweeps the Cutie Mark Crusaders up into the air. When it returns them to the ground, they discover that they now have...their cutie marks!

"Our cutie mark is the Cutie Mark Crusaders emblem!" they all shout.

When Rarity, Applejack, and Rainbow Dash see that the Cutie Mark Crusaders have their cutie marks, they are overcome with tears of joy. They throw a big party to celebrate, and everypony comes! Yay!

Sweetie Belle, Apple Bloom, and Scootaloo now know that their special talent is to help other ponies understand their cutie marks. Cutie Mark Crusaders forever!

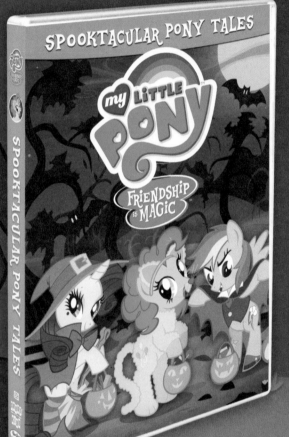